World of Enchantment: Legends & Myths

An International Collection of Children's Art

Foghorn Press
BOOKS BUILDING COMMUNITY

9 780935 701685

50995

Foghorn Press, Inc.
555 De Haro Street, Suite #220
San Francisco, CA 94107
Telephone 415/241-9550 or 800/FOGHORN
Fax 415/241-9648

Proceeds from *World of Enchantment: Legends & Myths* go to Paintbrush Diplomacy and the San Francisco Bay Area Book Council for funding its literacy programs and the annual Junior Publishers Program. Inquiries about the Junior Publishers Program may be addressed to:

San Francisco Bay Area Book Council
555 De Haro Street, Suite #220
San Francisco, CA 94107
Telephone 415/861-BOOK
Fax 415/241-9648

ISBN 0-935701-68-0

Distributed to the book trade by Publishers Group West in Emeryville, California. To contact your local sales representative, call 800/788-3123.

Cover art by Takashi Touma, Age 9, Japan **Ushiwakamaru and Benkei**

The representation or non-representation of certain countries in this book depended on the availability of artwork, and in no way reflects the political opinions of Foghorn Press, Paintbrush Diplomacy, the San Francisco Bay Area Book Council or the Junior Publishers Program.

Due to space constraints and the need for clarity, we have summarized many of the stories that accompany artwork. Wherever possible, we have included direct quotes from the artists. We have tried to retain the artists' original meaning and regret any misrepresentation.

The Editors

Mithu Bodak
Age 13
India

Untitled

World of Enchantment: Legends & Myths

An International Collection of Children's Art

Foghorn Press
BOOKS BUILDING COMMUNITY

Dibyendu Sett, Age 13, India   *Holiday Spots*

About Paintbrush Diplomacy

Paintbrush Diplomacy—it's a simple idea. Yet it can affect—and has already touched—youth from every corner of the earth. The brainchild of Char and Rudy Pribuss, Paintbrush Diplomacy fosters international communication through the exchange of children's art and letters. Children from China can learn about their peers in California. Teenagers in Kenya find common interests with students from New York.

Paintbrush Diplomacy is a not-for-profit organization that was founded in 1972. The contacts established over the past 21 years have created a worldwide communication network for children. We plan to open an International Children's Art Museum in San Francisco in 1994. Our permanent collection consists of 3,500 paintings from 80 countries.

Each year the International School Art and Letter Exchange Program chooses a new theme. In academic school year 1992-1993, the theme was "Fairy Tales, Fables, Epics, and Legends from Around the World" with more than 16,000 children participating. The artwork used in this publication was collected through this program. As you look through the book I am sure you will be inspired by the wealth of legends and myths from all over the world.

Paintbrush Diplomacy would like to thank all of the artists who participated and the Junior Publishers, as well as Foghorn Press and the Book Council for making this publication possible.

Germaine Juneau
Executive Director
Paintbrush Diplomacy

Paintbrush Diplomacy Staff:
Germaine Juneau, Executive Director
Andrew Hunter, Former Director of School Programs
Diane Goloff, Director of School Programs
Nanette Tver, Development Officer

Introduction

The Third Annual Junior Publishers Program, sponsored by the San Francisco Bay Area Book Council, proudly presents the publication of *World of Enchantment: Legends & Myths —An International Collection of Children's Art.*

There are 19 of us who belong to this program. We range in age from 14 to 18 and are from culturally diverse backgrounds, each bringing our own unique skills and perspectives. During six weeks of our summer vacation we edited, produced, marketed, lunched, faxed, and sent out press releases. We ran a publishing house and produced this incredible book!

World of Enchantment: Legends & Myths contains 85 selections submitted by young artists from Argentina, Bangladesh, Japan, the United States, and dozens of other countries. The artwork and stories were collected by Paintbrush Diplomacy and revolved around this year's theme of fantasies, myths and legends. This is not an art book, nor a storybook; it is a delightful combination of both.

We are VERY excited about the publication of our book. We have worked amazingly hard over these last six weeks and we have learned so much. The project involved a lot of teamwork, bickering, decision making, and ultimately great satisfaction. We wish to thank those who took the time to help us, as well as all the young artists who contributed their work. And a special thanks to Paintbrush Diplomacy, our almighty publisher Foghorn Press, and the San Francisco Bay Area Book Council, the sponsor of the entire program.

The 1993 Junior Publishers

Santanu Das, Age 12, India   *The Farmer and His Sons*

Sakiko Shioya, Age 12, Japan   *Gombei the Wild Duck Hunter*

About the Junior Publishers Program

Every year as June and the launch of the Junior Publishers Program approach, I have my doubts. Can this year's junior publishers pull it off? Can a group of teenagers who know nothing about publishing actually learn enough in the course of a six-week program to put a book together? Can the "great art of publishing" be performed by beginners?

When the 1993 Junior Publishers Program began, it was immediately clear that the kids were exceptional. I found myself racing to keep up with 19 astonishing and energetic "beginner" minds. After they found their places in the publishing company, in either the production, editorial or marketing department, they called a meeting with me. They let me know that in order to best feature the art of this wonderful book, they would require color throughout and a larger format than in previous years' books. I reviewed the budget. It did not allow for either. Then I looked at the art. Our commitment to the project grew and the budget was adjusted upward.

The lessons came to the instructors as much as to the junior publishers. As "the professionals," we struggled not to interfere, and to guide only when necessary. As one parent pointed out to me, this is a challenge not unlike parenting. Beginners excel because of their willingness to challenge and risk. The 1993 junior publishers are to be congratulated for challenging themselves and each other over the course of the program. Their work and their heart have resulted in this stunning achievement—the book itself.

So, with the publication of this book, my doubts again have been dispelled. For that I have the junior publishers to thank and I warmly do so.

Vicki K. Morgan
President, San Francisco Bay Area Book Council
Publisher, Foghorn Press

Foreword
by **Robert D. San Souci**, author of *Cut From the Same Cloth: American Women of Myth, Legend and Tall Tales* and *Short and Shivery: 30 Ghostly Stories Retold From World Folk Literature*

The book you are holding is a unique gathering of artwork from young people around the world. These accomplished artists illustrate their favorite myths and legends, folk tales and fairy tales. Through drawings or paintings, each artist shares a part of him or herself, provides a glimpse of his or her culture, and reminds us that children (and adults) everywhere are fascinated with the marvelous characters and creatures of the imagination. These paintings reaffirm our universality while celebrating the unique vision of the individual and of individual cultures. This is "paintbrush diplomacy" at its finest.

Folklorists especially prize materials that pass from a native artist or storyteller directly to the viewer or listener, without a lot of editing or commentary. This is what *World of Enchantment* provides. The contributors share firsthand the colorful images that have leapt like an electric spark from their imaginations to their canvases. Some artists show a remarkable grasp of technique; others have a raw, untutored energy. But all of them have the power to bring alive the fabulous creatures that populate the myths and tales that fire their imaginations.

The artists—from China, Greece, Bulgaria, India, the United States, Poland, Japan and many other countries—present a rich diversity of mythic figures. Pandora, the Goddess Durga, Puss in Boots, Hopi Katchinas, Ushiwakamaru and Benkei, and others come alive in art that captures the drama of the tales while providing glimpses of the history, everyday life, religious beliefs, and literature of numerous peoples.

Each illustration is a small miracle, compressing a vital part of a unique culture into a single, dynamic image. The book itself is also a wonder, produced entirely by the junior publishers. I had the pleasure of meeting these young people and viewing their promising "work in progress." That the completed book fulfills that promise is no surprise, given their abundant talents. They have made a valuable contribution to the cause of promoting understanding among all peoples.

bask yourself in myth

Mythology, stretching your liquid arms
Sunlight glistening over a troubled sea, a ray of hope exuding.
Myths and life rise with the tide, overflowing gently, slowly,
to far corners of the earth.
We have only to laugh in the face of adversity,
reach out our arms, and gather the sea.
The beauty of myth, pounding on far-flung shores,
we need only collect it to experience the wonder.
Myth makes us as a people all the richer.
Down pounds the surf.
Bask yourself in myth, in joy.

by Gabriel Caffrey, age 15 (1993 Junior Publisher)

Farzana Sohel, Age 13, Bangladesh   **The Rainbow, The Fairy and The Lotus Girl**

Table of Contents

We would like to dedicate this book to the human race,
in the hope that our contribution to understanding each other
will help us live together happily ever after.

1993 Junior Publishers

Wynne Lawrence, Age 9, Australia *The Python*

The Python story takes place during the Dreamtime, near the Liverpool River in Australia.

"Long ago during the Dreamtime, there lived Turramulli, the Giant Quinkin. He lived in Cape York. One day when he was hungry, he went into the Yalannji village looking for food. As he walked into town, his feet made a loud *"wock, wock, wock"* sound, which frightened the Yalannji people into running away. When the Turramulli threatened to eat two village children, the Timara Quinkins reached out their long arms and pulled the children to safety."

Mitchell Smith, Age 9, Australia
Turramulli The Giant Quinkin

"Long ago there was a King who wanted a child. He married seven times, but only his last wife was kind. Because of her kindness, an old pious man blessed her so that she could have children. A year later, she had seven sons and one daughter, named Parul.

The six older Queens became jealous of her fertility. They chased her away to the forest, killed all of her sons, and buried them in the garden. Where they were buried, a tree named Champa grew. But Parul survived and was raised by the gardener's wife as her own daughter.

A. K. M. Pavel Rahman, Age 13, Bangladesh   *Seven Brothers' Champa*

As Parul grew up, she often took walks in the garden and heard the trees cry out her name, "Parul, Parul!" Later, she found out the story of her brothers and her mother from the gardener's wife.

Meanwhile, Parul met a Prince and they fell in love. Hearing the story from her, he gave her a magic mirror, in which she could see her mother wandering all alone in the forest. A few days later, Parul was to sing for the harvest festival. She sang the story of what happened to her brothers and her mother. The King, who was in the audience, was astonished to hear that Parul was his daughter. The kind Queen was brought from the forest and together they all went to the Champa tree. The brothers trapped inside told Parul that they would be free if the evil Queens begged forgiveness of their mother. The Queens did as they were asked and then were driven from the palace. The King, Queen and children lived happily ever after."

Teresa Mustafiz, Age 12, Bangladesh   *In The Fairy Land of Flowers*

"Runy, Thunu and their friends were surprised to see the beautiful birds, the trees and the colorful butterflies in the Fairy Land of Flowers. The gorgeous fairy landed, welcomed them and invited them to eat. The children were stunned to see that the trees were not only filled with flowers, but also with delicious food. They climbed the trees and plucked the flowers."

Dimitar Kiriakov, Age 11, Bulgaria *Buratino*

Elena Dimova, Age 9, Bulgaria *Survakari*

Page 6—
Maria Baltadzieva, Age 11, Bulgaria *Kukeri*

Page 7—
Georgi Kisov, Age 11, Bulgaria *Kukeri*

Tahia Radeva, Age 12, Bulgaria *The Water Ghost*

This story is about a slave who was chosen by the King to inherit the throne.

Artist Unknown,
Burkina Faso

The Slave Enthroned

Gao Lin, Age 8, China *The Door Geniuses*

Gao Lin, Age 8, China *Untitled*

梅花

光亚小学

二唐思彦

九三年春

Sei Jun Tang, China   *Plum Blossom*

Lucie Sinkmajerova, Age 12, Czech Republic   *The Trojan Horse*

𝕒 famous symbol of the Trojan War was the Trojan Horse. The Greeks hid in this hollow wooden horse and secretly gained entry to the city of Troy. At night, they came out of the horse and lay siege to Troy. In this way, they won the war.

Jiri Pikrt and Filip Dostail, Age 11, Czech Republic   *Prince Bajaja*

Next page: Veronika Tucimova, Age 12, Czech Republic   *The Magician Zito*

"*One* day, the Devil decided he wanted to marry a certain orphan girl. The girl was having a bath when the Devil entered her room. She told the Devil that since she had no clothes on and owned no jewels, she could not marry him. He brought her what she needed, so that she would be forced to marry him even though she did not want to. Just as the girl came out to marry the Devil, the rooster began to crow. Since the Devil could not bear the rooster's crowing, he had to leave and the girl did not have to marry him."

Marili Sokk, Estonia   **Night-Time Suitor**

"*This* is a story about a kettle of money, which appears only once every one hundred years. These lucky men happened to be in the right place at the right time."

Evelin Parnamets, Age 15, Estonia   **A Kettle of Money**

Three sisters were kidnapped when they were just babies by an old and evil Witch.

Everyday, she made them spin golden yarn from morning until night. Many years later, a Prince came along and fell in love with the youngest sister.

One day, when the Witch was not at home, he decided to take the girl to his palace. As the Witch was returning, she saw them escaping. She was furious and sent a cursed ball after them. The ball hit their horse and the girl fell into a nearby river and turned into a water lily.

With the Wizard's help, the Prince was able to defeat the Witch and rescue the three sisters, and they all lived happily ever after.

Mari Loit, Estonia
Gold Spinners

Kally Halkia, Age 12, Greece **Centaur**

Nadia Beltzasian, Age 14, Greece **Against Two Snakes**

Ellie Tsirliagou, Age 13, Greece *Icarus and Daedalus*

The Greeks considered Daedalus to be the best and most talented craftsman, artist, architect and inventor. One day, King Minos, ruler of the island of Crete, asked Daedalus to build a labyrinth that would entrap the mighty monster, Minotaur. Daedalus built the labyrinth and the King praised him greatly. King Minos had a hair-trigger temper. So one day, when he was annoyed at Daedalus, he banished and imprisoned him with his son, Icarus, in a high tower on an island with many guards watching over it day and night. To escape, Daedalus put his talents to work and devised a plan. He gathered fallen feathers and made wings for him and his son. Daedalus gave his son very specific instructions on how to fly to freedom, but Icarus did not listen. Icarus fell into the ocean and drowned. Daedalus was very angry at himself for creating such an invention and decided to build a temple to honor the god Apollo. There he hung up his wings in memory of his son.

Pandora's Box is a Greek myth about a woman named Pandora. Her husband, Epimetheus, owned a large box which held all of the things that could harm humankind. He kept it in a special room that he forbade Pandora to enter.

Pandora became increasingly curious about the contents of the box, until one day she could no longer contain her insatiable curiosity. While her husband was sleeping, she stole his key and quietly entered the room where the box was stored. Pandora opened the box and all the evils of the world flew out. The only good thing that came out of the box was hope. Without hope we would not be able to survive all of the problems and misfortunes of the world.

Stauros Halkias, Age 12, Greece *Pandora's Box*

Barbara Toulkeridou, Age 14, Greece *The Argo*

"The *Argo* is the name of this boat with the distinctive and strange eye on the sail. Jason and the Argonauts went with this boat to Colchis. The ship was made with the help of the two Olympian goddesses, Athena and Hera. Athena placed the wood of a prophetic tree inside the boat, so the boat had the ability to see the future. *The Argo* had fifty paddles and was so light that the Argonauts could carry it when they were on land."

Nirmallya Roy, Age 16, India   *Holiday Spots (Victoria Memorial)*

Dhruv Khanna, Age 12, India *Krishna*

Asfak Ali Begg, Age 13, India *Immersion of Goddess Durga*

"This picture is taken from the great Indian epic, the Mahabharata. In the epic, Krishna, our Indian God, was very fond of butter when he was little. Whenever his mother, Yashoda, was churning butter for the family, he liked to eat from the barrel. In this picture, Krishna is asking his mother for some of the butter she is churning. When his mother refuses to give him some of it, Krishna tries persuading her and she loses her patience."

Somanko Pal, Age 11, India **The Divine Eye**

"My painting, titled 'The Divine Eye,' depicts a painter putting to form the image of Goddess Kali, ready for worship."

Pranav Goenka, Age 14, India **A Widow's Savings**

Raghav Kanoria, Age 14, India *Bheema and Hanuman*

Asfak Ali Begg, Age 13, India *A Hare's Devotion*

"*Once* there was a Monk and a Hare who lived in a cave. One winter it was too cold for them to go out to search for food and so they became weak from hunger.

The devoted Hare asked the Monk to take his flesh so that he could survive the harsh winter. The Monk refused such a hard proposal, but the Hare insisted again and again. The Hare said, "My Lord, it is my duty to save my Master's life, so please promise that you will take my flesh after my death."

When at last the Hare got the Monk's assurance, the Hare jumped into the fire. As he promised, the Monk took his flesh and was saved. He blessed the Hare's soul, "May your soul be in peace in the moon for eternal life."

Since then, the moon is identified as Shashadhar, Holder of the Hare.""

"Shibi, a legendary Indian King, grew so powerful by virtue of his divine qualities that the Gods, shaken with the fear of losing their kingdom, decided to test his nobility and bring out the weakness in him.

One day, a terrible-looking eagle entered the royal court chasing after a little dove. The trembling dove was at once sheltered in the King's robe.

When the angry eagle demanded its prey, the King replied calmly, "I cannot betray the trust of a refugee but you will be served any other food you choose."

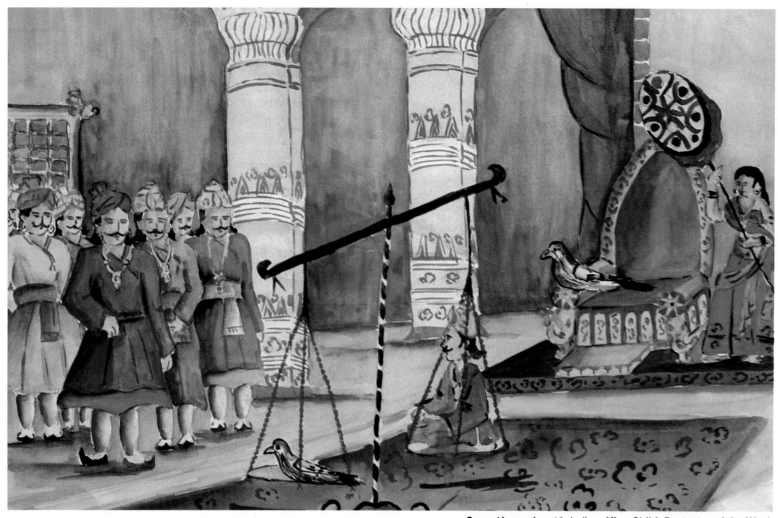

Soma Konar, Age 13, India   *King Shibi, Protector of the Weak*

The eagle retorted mockingly, "Then I choose your flesh equal to the weight of the dove."

The King agreed without a second thought. Surprisingly, the balance continued to show the dove heavier than the King's flesh. In order to make the sides equal, the King at last sat on the scale.

Enchanted by his self-sacrifice, Indra, the Chief of the Gods, and Agni, the God of Fire, appeared in the place of the eagle and the dove. They blessed the King and declared, "You deserve homage even from Gods."

"*While* traveling in a forest, three dishonest men found a purse filled with money. They agreed to divide the money amongst themselves. As they were very hungry, one of them went to buy some food in town. After he bought the food, he poisoned it so that he could keep all of the money. During his absence his two partners became greedy and decided to murder the first man so they could divide the money between them. When the first man came back, the other two attacked and killed him. Then they began eating the food that the first man had bought. As the food was full of poison, they died as well. In the end none of the wicked men got any of the money. The moral is: Greed is bad for you."

Atreyee Chakrabarty, Age 12, India ***Three Greedy Men***

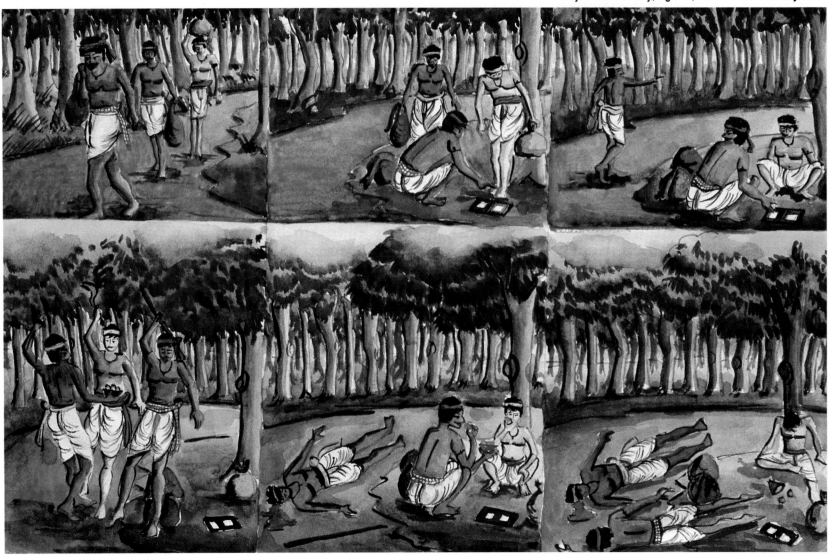

Shibantayan Mallick III, Age 9, India
Too Much Greed Leads To Death

Once upon a time, an old crane could not catch fish, so he planned cleverly. He spread a rumor that a pond was drying up. The fish panicked. They came to the crane and said, "Sir, please carry us to another pond." The crane was pleased and carried one fish after another, but he ate them. One day a crab came. The crane was happy for a change in the menu, so he carried the crab to his favorite lunch place. When the crab saw the pile of fish bones there, he realized his fate. He immediately pressed his claws around the crane's throat and killed him.

During the evening, it is an old Hindu custom to pray to the Goddess for peace.

Ayan Panja, Age 9, India ***A Hindu Woman***

27

Takamasa Wakumoto, Age 9, Japan *Peach Boy Taro*

Asami Seki, Age 9, Japan *The Flower Bloomer*

This is from an ancient Japanese legend, *Tsuru No Ongaeshi*. On a cold winter day, a poor old woodcutter released a crane that was caught in a trap. The next day, the old man and his wife were rewarded for this deed with a beautiful girl, who appeared on their doorstep to live with them. To repay her new parents for their kindness, the girl wanted to weave beautiful cloth for them to sell, on the condition that no one watch her work. The girl weaved for three days and three nights straight. The old man, however, was very curious and peeked into the girl's room. He was shocked to see a crane sitting on a loom, plucking out her feathers to weave into cloth! But now that her parents knew her secret, the girl could not live with them anymore. As a crane, she flew away forever.

Once upon a time, an old man and an old woman were living in a country village in Japan. They were poor and spent each day weaving big straw hats to sell in nearby towns.

New Years was approaching, and the old couple wanted to have rice cakes to celebrate. So the next day, the old man went into town with five new hats. Unfortunately, he did not sell a single one. As he was trudging wearily back home, it began to snow. While walking up a mountain trail, he suddenly came upon a row of six statues of Jizo, the Protector of Children, who repre-

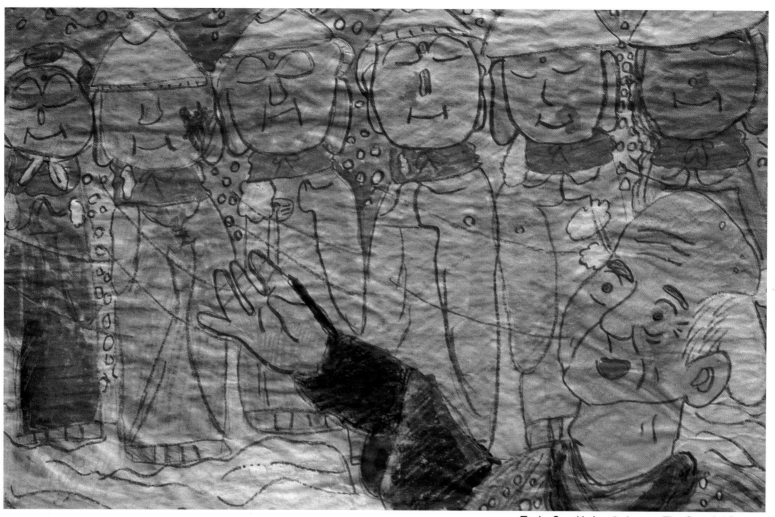

Taeko Suzuki, Age 8, Japan *The Grateful Statues*

sented kindness, love and sincerity. Even though they were just statues, the old man thought they must have been cold. So he tied his five hats onto five of the six statues. Then he took off his own and put it on the last Jizo.

When he arrived home, the old man apologized to his wife for not bringing back any rice cakes for New Years. He explained how he gave away the five hats, as well as his own, to the six Jizo statues. His wife was very proud of him and believed that performing this kind deed was far better than having all the rice cakes in the world.

Just before dawn the next day, the old couple was awakened by the chanting of voices: *"A kind old man walking in the snow gave all his hats to the stone Jizo. So we bring him gifts with a yo-heave-ho!"*

When they opened the door to see who was there, the couple were surprised to discover on their doorstep a straw mat with a big, scrumptious rice cake neatly arranged on top. In the distance, they saw the six Jizo statues marching home, the hats still on top of their heads. As a result of the old man's kindness and generosity, the couple had a wonderful New Years celebration.

Kiyoshi Takasu, Age 12, Japan *Gombei—the Wild Duck Hunter*

These are scenes from the Japanese tale of *Kamotori Gombei*. Gombei was a man who made his living by hunting wild ducks. One day, however, he had the adventure of his life. On this day, a series of odd events occurred. Gombei caught over one hundred ducks, compared to his normal catch of three or four.

Then he accidentally caught a wild boar and a rabbit, things he never caught before. Later, his amazing luck changed. Gombei got sprayed by a whale and then became a target for a group of hungry sharks. He was also picked up by wild ducks, who dropped him off onto the roof of a high pagoda!

Yuuko Niibori, Age 12, Japan *Gombei—the Wild Duck Hunter*

Yumi Osada, Age 10, Japan *Kaguyahime*

This is an illustration from the tale of *Kaguyahime,* which means "Beautiful Princess." She is being carried off to the moon by angels, who wish to turn her into an angel as well.

Yuki Kimura, Age 9, Japan *The Flower Bloomer*

Peter Otieno, Age 17, Kenya   *Nyamgotho and the Woman of the Lake*

34

*L*ong ago there was a young man named Nyamgotho, who lived alone on a lake shore. He fished a lot, but usually he did not catch anything.

One evening he sat on the rocks as he watched the sunset. He asked the ancestors of the lake to give him a woman who would help him around his house.

The next day, Nyamgotho awoke to hear noises of goats, cows, sheep and hens. He dashed out of his hut and was shocked to see a beautiful young woman standing in front of him, soaking wet.

He ran back inside to retrieve a soft towel and some hot tea. She tasted the tea and immediately spat it out and said that the tea was the worst she ever had. After she dried herself, she went in the hut and began cooking.

The next morning, Nyamgotho awoke to find that his slum had turned into a king's castle. The woman had prepared everything for him, even his fishing net and boat. That evening, as he watched the sunset, an old man's voice cautioned him not to mistreat her—OR ELSE. Then a dark brown stick arose out of the lake and he was told to never release the stick.

In time, he became a drunk and irresponsible man. He sold all the cows and the other livestock, even though they belonged to the woman.

Some nights he would return home very drunk. The stick was magic so it would lead him back home. One night he came home late and found her sitting by the fire. He asked her for food and she explained there wasn't any. He took a firm grip of the magic stick and started to beat her.

The next morning he woke to see that the woman and all her belongings were returning to the lake. He carried his stick and went outside to stop her. Even the livestock he had sold were returning and disappearing into the lake. He raced in front of the woman and tried to stop her but she continued to march towards the lake.

Nyamgotho got angry, and as he hit her head with the magic stick, he began to transform into a tree. He did not leave the magic stick because he thought it would help him.

To this very day Nyamgotho's tree is still there holding the magic stick. No one touches it because it is bad luck.

Once upon a time, there was a very beautiful girl named Wahera. Many young men in her village admired her and proposed to her, but she said that she would only marry the man who managed to get for her the tail of a giant Linani monster. Many young men tried this, but in vain because the monsters were very strong and wild.

One day a brave man by the name of Namtando decided to try his luck. He set off to the country of the giant monsters and waited until nightfall. When all of the giants were asleep, he quickly cut off the tail of one of the Linani monsters. Namtando then ran off, happy that he had earned the hand of the beautiful Wahera.

Ogulla Conrad, Age 16, Kenya **The Bride Who Wanted a Special Present**

Ronald Orucho, Age 17, Kenya **The Legend**

A slave was very clever and got out of a deadly situation and to safety. He did this by tying himself to an eagle's foot and escaping from a poisonous snake's lair. Through his cleverness, he escaped from slavery.

Njoroge Duncan, Age 16, Kenya   *How the Zebra Got Its Stripes*

Long ago, donkeys were the only work animals people had. Some of the donkeys attempted to run away to escape cruelty. The hare painted some donkeys with stripes to hide them, and they ran away. To this day, the ones that escaped are known as zebras.

Milda Valaviciute, Age 12, Lithuania *Queen Egle of the Snakes*

"The mushrooms decided to go to war. They were very courageous and proud. But a child came to the forest and buried all the mushrooms."

Rolandas Stanevicius, Age 9, Lithuania
The War of Mushrooms

Mindaugas Ambrasas, Age 11, Lithuania
Gediminas' Dream

Antanas Laurynas, Age 11, Lithuania
The Man and the Devil

Milda Valaviciute, Age 12, Lithuania
Yurate and Kastytis

Next page: Sarunas Sirvinskas, Age 9, Lithuania   *The Tom Cat and the Cock*

Marija Tyminskyte, Lithuania *12 Brothers Who Were Turned into Ravens*

Once upon a time, there was a man who had two wives. One was very poor and the other was rich. Each wife had a baby. One day, the poor wife took her child with her to the forest. When she got to the woods, she laid her baby at the foot of a big tree while she gathered leaves to sell for money. While she was looking for leaves, a huge bird came and carried away her child. When she saw that her baby had disappeared, she began to cry. Then she looked up and saw the giant bird holding her baby. With tears in her eyes, she begged the bird to return her child to her. The bird told her, "You are very poor. I shall give you plenty of money and clothes, but I shall not give you your child back." The woman cried, "Dear bird, I don't want money or clothes. All I want is my baby. I can spend all your money and your clothes

Olatunji Peter Adewale, Age 15, Nigeria *A Nursing Mother and the Bird*

will get old, but I will always have my child." The bird took pity on the poor woman. He returned her child and gave her money and clothes, also. When the poor wife returned home, she told the rich wife what had happened and shared the bird's gifts with her.

The rich wife was greedy and wanted to get some money and clothes from the bird for herself. So the next day she dressed her baby in beautiful clothes and went to the forest. She put her baby at the foot of the same tree, and walked away to find some leaves. When she returned, her baby was still on the ground. She looked up and said, "Oh bird, please I beg you to take away this child and give me plenty of money and beautiful clothes in return. This baby is too much trouble for me, and I'd rather be rich."

In response, the bird cried loudly, "Go away, and take your baby with you. You are a very greedy woman who does not deserve beautiful clothes and riches."

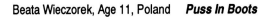

Once upon a time there lived an old miller who had three sons, a donkey, and a cat. When the old miller died, his first son took the windmill, his second son took the donkey, and his third son was left with the cat. The cat wanted to make his master rich, so he asked to be taken to the shoemaker to have a pair of boots made for him.

When the cat received his boots, he ran into the forest and caught some partridges, the king's favorite meal, and brought them to the palace. The king asked the cat who his master was, and he told him that his master was a count, although he was only a miller's son. When the cat returned home with the bag of gold, his master was very happy. The cat continued to bring the king sacks of partridges, and the king rewarded him kindly for each sack.

The king was so pleased with the cat's gifts that he wanted to meet his master. On the day that the cat and his master were to meet the king, the cat told his master to take a swim in the nearby lake. Confused, the miller's son agreed because he trusted the cat since he had brought him wealth. While his master was bathing, the cat hid his clothes. Then he ran to the king and told him that someone had stolen his master's clothes while he was bathing. The king gave the cat some of his own clothes for his master to wear. The poor miller's son now had clothes that made him look like royalty.

Meanwhile, the cat ran off in search of other ways to help his master trick the king. The cat saw some beautiful fields and meadows where poor peasants were working diligently. When he asked them who owned the land, they told him that an evil wizard did. Then the cat went to the wizard's fortress and tricked the wizard into changing himself into a mouse. As soon as he did, the cat gobbled him up and that was the end of the evil wizard.

When the king saw the evil wizard's land, he thought that it was extremely beautiful. The cat greeted him and said that the fortress belonged to his master, the count. The king was astonished and impressed with the fortress that was even larger and more attractive than his own palace.

When the king's daughter met the now wealthy miller's son,

This is a story about a small boy who hates animals. One day a wizard comes to him and changes him into a Lilliputian, a person so small he could ride on the back of a duck. Ashamed, the boy starts on a long journey to find the wizard to help change him back. He has a lot of very interesting, and sometimes dangerous adventures on his way to the wizard. After a few years, the boy returns home and the wizard changes him back to normal. But from then on, he respects and loves all animals, because he now understands them."

Ylasia Waliszeuslia, Poland
Wonderful Travels of Nicols Anderson

Patricia Schafer, Age 9, Poland
The Story About a Foolish John

she thought he was very handsome and the two soon got married. The miller's son became a real count and took over the evil wizard's land and fortress. The fields and meadows that once belonged to the evil wizard were now filled with happiness and festivity.

When the king fell ill and died, the count was chosen to be the new king. The miller's son remembered his faithful Puss in Boots who helped him so much, by making him Lord Chamberlain over his court, and they all lived happily ever after.

This story is about the fox and the grapes. One day the fox was hungry as he was walking through a meadow. High above his head, hanging from vines, he saw some delicious-looking grapes. First he tried jumping to reach them, then knocking them down, but the grapes were just too high. Finally, after all his efforts failed, he decided he didn't want them, as the grapes were probably sour anyway.

Jose Carlos Goncalves, Age 15, Portugal
The Fox and the Grapes

Lena, Age 12, Russia *Untitled*

Lukyanova Yana, Age 11, Russia *Untitled*

Denis, Age 10, Russia *Untitled*

Olga, Age 12, Russia *The Dragon*

"Don't leave me, bring me to the stepmother" said the skull.

Dasha, Russia
Vasilia the Beautiful

"The King of the Sky had seven beautiful daughters who were called the "Seven Angels." They danced and sang and their father loved them very much."

Gua Ling Ng, Age 13, Taiwan   **Seven Angels**

"Na Zha was the daughter of a genie who was called Li Qing. Li Qing was clever and lovely. She could fight very well and defeat all the soldiers in the sea."

Wei Zhong Xiu, Age 9, Taiwan
Na Zha—Rollicked in the Sea of the East

"Oh! It is so scary! A tiger made himself look like the grandmother of a little boy. The disguised tiger knocked on the little boy's door. The boy thought it was his grandmother, so he opened the door. The disguised tiger came into the house and ate the boy's younger brother.

The little boy's sister was so angry that she climbed up a tree outside and lured the tiger out. When the tiger was directly below her, she burned it with a wok full of boiling oil.

This story teaches you that when you come across a danger, you have to be composed in order to get away from it."

Si Yuen Jeng, Age 7, Taiwan   *Tiger Grandmother*

Yi Chuan Hung, Taiwan   *Brandishing the Lion*

Christie Boone, Age 13, USA
Buffalo Woman

"*One* day, a young man who hunts buffalo meets a beautiful young woman from the Buffalo Nation. They are married and have a son named Call Boy. But the young man's family is cruel to his wife and chase her and her son away. When the young man returns from hunting and finds out what happened, he follows their tracks. He finds them in a tipi and stays the night, but they are gone with the tipi the next morning. This happens again the next day when he follows them.

After several days, he tracks them but finds the buffalo of the Buffalo Nation instead of the tipi. The buffalo inform him that he will be killed if he stays, but the young man refuses to leave his wife and son. The chief lines up all the buffalo and tells the man to pick his family from among them. He can, because he knows his son flicks his left ear and his wife has a burr on her back. The buffalo are impressed. They let him live and turn him into a buffalo so he can stay with his wife and son."

Erica Pacheco, Age 13, USA *Sir Walter and the Dragon*

"My drawing is about Sir Walter and the Dragon. He thought he could surprise the Dragon at night but, oh well! Poor Sir Walter, burned to a crisp by the Dragon's fire!"

"*My* picture is of the Hodag who lived in the northern woods of Wisconsin. The lumberjacks were scared of the Hodag because when he came out of his den to roam the forest, the floor rumbled and he knocked down all the trees in sight."

Justin Graf, Age 10, USA
The Hodag

Philip Huh, Age 12, USA
The Simpleton

"My favorite story is called 'Brother Eagle, Sister Sky.' It is a message from a Native American man named Chief Seattle. The main character in this story is the earth, and the moral is that if we do not take care of our earth then we will have no place to live."

Shalynn Chambliss, Age 13, USA   ***Brother Eagle, Sister Sky***

Clayton Strasburg, Age 11, USA
Gulliver's Travels

Burgundy Tyrrel, Age 8, USA
The Three Little Pigs

Once there was a woman who had a constant longing for a fruit called rapunzel. This fruit was found only in the Witch's forbidden garden. The woman's husband loved her so much that despite the danger, he often stole rapunzels from the garden.

One fateful day, as he was climbing over the wall, the Witch grabbed his ankles. As punishment for stealing her fruit, they had to give the Witch their first-born child. When a baby girl was finally born, the Witch took her away, named her "Rapunzel," and locked her up in a high tower with one window and no stairs. Rapunzel grew up to become a beautiful but lonely young woman with long golden hair. Whenever the Witch wanted to see her she called out, "Rapunzel, Rapunzel, let down your long hair," and she climbed up to the top of the tower, using Rapunzel's hair as a rope.

One day a Prince rode through the forest and heard Rapunzel singing. He liked the sound of her voice so much that he returned the next day. As he hid in the bushes listening to Rapunzel's song, he saw the Witch yelling at her to let down her hair. After the Witch had left, the Prince decided to try it himself.

Rapunzel let down her hair and the Prince climbed up. At first, she was scared because she had never seen a man before, but he calmed her down. They decided that some night they would sneak away by climbing down a ladder that Rapunzel would weave with her hair. The old Witch remained unaware of Rapunzel's plot, until one day, Rapunzel mentioned to her: "The Prince is heavier to lift up than you are." Without delay, the Witch cut off Rapunzel's hair.

When the Prince came to steal Rapunzel away, the Witch was ready. She hung the braids out the window, and when he had almost reached the top, the Witch dropped him. The Prince fell down and his eyes were pierced by thorns. Heartbroken, Rapunzel leaped out of the window but amazingly, she was not hurt. Rapunzel cried for her beloved Prince, and her tears fell into his eyes. Magically, he could see again. While Rapunzel and the Prince were running away, the old Witch could not get out of the tower. She grew smaller and smaller until she was the size of an apple. Then a huge raven came and carried her away to her nest, and she was never seen again. The Prince took Rapunzel and made her the Queen of his kingdom.

Kendra Bulgrin, Age 11, USA   *Rapunzel*

"*In* the Hopi (Native American) tradition,
Nuvakchina means 'Snow Kachina.'
You might see him in the Bean Dance,
the Water Serpent Dance, or the Mixed Kachina Dance."

Lizzie Ebert, Age 11, USA   *Nuvakchina*

Michael Tan, Age 15, USA
The Wild Swans

"My picture is about a famous logger named Paul Bunyan.
He was a huge man and had a blue ox named Babe.
Paul could cut down eight trees at one time, and
Babe could pull one million logs in one tug."

Jeremy Ryan, Age 11, USA   *Paul Bunyan and His Blue Ox Named Babe*

"*For* my picture I chose to draw an Indian girl. It represents the Native Americans who were the first people in our country. The land originally belonged to them and they have had a great influence on our country."

Heather Clark, Age 16, USA *Indian Girl*

"*This* is a picture of myself as an American Indian Chief. I did this because I have great respect for the Indians, and have some Indian ancestry."

Christopher Rausch, Age 16, USA *Indian Chief*

61

Once upon a time, there was a mysterious man named Helanzer who was deeply in love with a princess named Alangica. Helanzer had no money, in fact, he hardly had anything. He only saw Alangica when the moon was out, in back of her palace. When Alangica asked where he lived and who his family was, Helanzer always replied, "When the time comes, I will tell you all that needs to be told." Alangica was very stubborn and impatient, and even though her love for Helanzer was great, she refused to see him anymore unless he told her the details of his very mysterious life. With great reluctance, Alangica stopped meeting Helanzer in the evenings, and soon forgot all about him.

Three years later, Alangica was to marry a young prince. Everyone seemed pleased with the match. On the wedding day, among the brightly wrapped packages lay a discolored leaf. Frowning with displeasure, Alangica picked up the leaf to throw it away. Just as she was disposing of it, she noticed a short message scratched onto the leaf:

Your biggest present of all awaits you in the forest.
Your Lover, Helanzer

Alangica wondered who in the kingdom would play a stupid trick like this, when all of sudden an overwhelming urge to look in the forest came over her. As she ran through the woods, her heart felt as though it would burst through her chest. Alangica never made it back to her wedding. No trace was ever found of her except for the following note:

We went to a place where we won't be judged by our looks, our wealth, or our race.

Helanzer and Alangica

Most people thought that the note was just a joke, until they realized that she would never return.

Callie Koers, Age 14, USA
The Legend of the Man in the Forest

Danny Castro, Age 12, USA   *Babe the Blue Ox Standing*

Index by Artist's Country

Index by Artist's Name

1993 Junior Publishers at the post-program celebration party

Top Row: Sharon Treece (instructor), Victoria Oswald (assistant instructor), Dion Wilson (Associate Publisher), Vicki Morgan (program director), Amanda Howard (Publisher), Rodney Brown (Assistant Marketing Director), Jon Grout (Marketing Director)

Middle Row: Angie Byun (Production Manager), Nia Fong in lion suit (Copy Editor), Gabriel Caffrey (Assistant Managing Editor), Alicia Roca (Publicity Manager), Nicole Wong (Event Coordinator), Francesca Bing-Yin Yee (Desktop Publisher), Tannie Soo Hoo (Copy Editor), Natasha Ong (Writer/Section Editor), Meka Shea Hall (Desktop Publisher), Chanda Willis (Desktop Publisher)

Bottom Row: Daniel Burton (Illustrator), Tyrone Dangerfield (Publicist), Jennifer Lyn French (Art Director)

Not pictured: Christopher Wu (Sales Manager/Publicist) and Stefanni Akib-Armstrong (Managing Editor)

Junior Publishers Program Staff Biographies

Stephanie Akib-Armstrong, 17, of Oakland, enjoys reading, writing, theater arts and music. In the fall of 1993, she will attend UCLA and pursue a career in creative writing and theater arts.

Rodney Brown, 17, of Oakland, loves music, sports and young ladies. An excellent writer, Rodney is the future sports editor for the *Fremont High Green & Gold* newspaper. His goal is to become president of his own advertising company.

Daniel Burton, 17, of Oakland, goes by the name of Chuck. He is an up-and-coming comic book artist who creates, writes and illustrates his own books. Computer graphics and design are two of his other hobbies.

Angie Byun, 17, of San Francisco, belongs to the Convent of the Sacred Heart High School student council and is an avid photographer. She hopes to study law or English and one day to become the first female Asian-American Senator.

Gabriel Caffrey, 15, of San Francisco, plans to follow a career in photography or writing. His interests include watching Star Trek, writing, photography and reading.

Tyrone Dangerfield, 16, of Oakland, enjoys writing about horror and sports. He aspires to become a director and writer of motion pictures.

Jennifer Lyn French, 15, of San Francisco, is an honors student at Lowell High School and has recently placed third in the National French Exam. She enjoys reading and drawing, and one day hopes to live in France and become fluent in five different languages.

Nia Fong, 16, of San Francisco, has been a reporter on *The Lowell* newspaper and has participated in badminton and basketball teams for the different schools she has attended. Nia hopes to someday live overseas.

Jon Grout, 16, of Washington state, is a novelist with one book under wraps and another on the way.

Meka Shea Hall, 15, of San Francisco, is very independent and hopes to become a successful business woman. She is studying to become one of the most gifted publishers in the state of California.

Amanda Howard, 17, of Berkeley, is Publicity Director for Kid Street Theatre, an organization that works to empower at-risk youth. She hopes to obtain a degree in international law, and to encourage women to enter into politics.

Natasha Ong, 14, of Redwood City, attends Notre Dame High School, and wishes to become a top anchorwoman as well as a famous magazine publisher.

Alicia Roca, 14, of San Francisco, aspires to be a well-known author. Her interests includes karate, art and journalism. Alicia also enjoys reading, painting and writing.

Tannie Soo Hoo, 17, of San Francisco, attends Lowell High School. Her varied interests include tennis, piano and reading. As a result of the Junior Publishers Program, she is interested in editing and writing as a possible career.

Chanda Willis, 16, of San Francisco, has credits from U.C. Berkeley and journalism training. She is talented at writing and desktop publishing.

Dion Wilson, 17, of Oakland, is an aficionado of the martial arts. He also aspires to be a professional comic book artist.

Nicole Wong, 14, of San Francisco, has won many awards for science projects and art posters and has served as vice-president for her school's student body. She hopes to become a Disney animator.

Christopher Wu, 16, of San Francisco, is a dedicated writer on his school newspaper, *The Lowell*. In his spare time, he enjoys listening to music.

Francesca Bing-Yin Yee, 18, of San Francisco, hopes to become an artist. She has won numerous prizes in drawing contests.

To order this book or previous Junior Publishers Program publications please contact:

Foghorn Press
555 De Haro Street
The Boiler Room, Suite #220
San Francisco, CA 94107
Telephone: 415/241-9550
or 800/FOGHORN

Proceeds from these books benefit the San Francisco Bay Area Book Council for use in funding its Junior Publishers Program and literacy programs in the Bay Area, as well as Paintbrush Diplomacy. The Junior Publishers publications include:

World of Enchantment: Legends and Myths—An International Collection of Children's Art, 1993
US $9.95/CAN $10.95/CAN with GST $11.45

Window to Our World—An International Collection of Kids' Art, 1992
US $5.99/CAN $6.99/CAN with GST $7.50

Books We Love Best—A Unique Guide to Children's Books, 1991
US $4.95/CAN $5.95/CAN with GST $6.45